# FOLK TALES
# FROM
# THE SOVIET
# UNION

Compiled by **Robert Babloyan** and **Mirlena Shumskaya**
Designed by **Mikhail Anikst**

# FOLK TALES FROM THE SOVIET UNION

## THE BALTIC REPUBLICS

**RADUGA PUBLISHERS**
**MOSCOW**

# CONTENTS

© Raduga Publishers 1986. Illustrated

ISBN 5-05-001559-6
ISBN 5-05-001562-6

# LATVIAN FOLK TALES

## The White Deer

Retold by *Lyudmila Kopylova*
Translated by *Fainna Solasko*
Illustrations by *Gunārs Krollis*

## The Sea Bride

Retold by *Lidiya Yeliseyeva*
Translated by *Kathleen Cook*
Illustrations by *Gunārs Krollis*

# THE WHITE DEER*

*Listen, and you shall hear,*
*This riddle is not long:*
*There was a great White Deer,*
*Its antlers were so strong.*
*Seen by everyone,*
*It was caught by none.*

Once upon a time there were two brothers. They grew up together as strong as two oaks by the river. One day their father said to them, "Tell me what trade you would choose."

His sons thought it over and then said, "We'd like to be carpenters. But we'd much rather be hunters and hunt geese and wild ducks."

Their father listened to what they said and then gave each son a bow and arrows and a good dog. He saw them to the gate and wished them good luck.

And so the brothers set out. After a while they came upon a flock of wild ducks. They both tried shooting their arrows, but did not hit anything. By then they discovered that they had wandered into a dense forest and could not find their way out. Although they had very little food left, they decided that come what may they would not lose heart.

Suddenly they spotted two antelopes. When the brothers raised their bows, the animals spoke to them in human voices. "Don't shoot us. We'll help you in time of need," they said.

So the brothers continued on their way. Soon they saw two wolves. They raised their bows, but the wolves said, "Don't shoot us. We'll help you in time of need."

They continued on their way once again. Soon they came upon two hares. The brothers raised their bows again, but the hares said, "Don't shoot us. We'll help you in time of need."

Thus did each of the brothers gain three true friends among the forest animals: an antelope, a grey wolf and a hare, to say nothing of their faithful dogs.

They went on until they came to a crossroads where they began to argue as to which road to take. Finally they decided that one would take one road and the other would take the other road and each would seek his own fortune. Before parting they decided that each of them would stick his knife into the trunk of an old oak. Later each would come back to the spot to see how his brother was faring. If his knife was shiny and sharp it meant he was making out well. If his knife was rusty it meant he was in trouble and needed his brother's help. They bid each other goodbye. One brother took the left road, while the other took the right road.

The elder brother walked on for a day and did not come upon anything. He walked on for a second day and did not come upon anything, either. Then, on the third day, he saw a hewn castle with the front and sides made of pine and the turret lost in the clouds. Though there was not a soul outside, a young maiden sat by the window.

"Tell me, pretty maiden, where has everyone gone?" the elder brother said.

"They went off to track the great White Deer, but they've all been turned into grey rocks and stones. My poor father was one of them."

"Don't worry, fair maiden. They went off without any

helpers, but see how many friends I have! They'll help me track the great White Deer, and I'll rescue your father as well."

The riddle was short, but the story is longer.

When the elder brother reached the gate he saw the great White Deer running by. He dashed after it with his antelope, grey wolf, dog and hare at his heels. But it was not as easy as he thought, for the White Deer simply vanished, with a faint haze to mark the spot where it had been.

An old hag sat by a fire at the edge of the forest nearby. The elder brother went up to her and said, "Will you let me warm myself by your fire, Granny?"

"Yes, do. You won't bother me. Just let me pat your beasties first. I shan't harm them."

"Go right ahead."

The moment the old hag touched the animals they turned to grey stones and rocks, as did the elder brother.

Meanwhile, the younger brother wandered back and forth in a great forest. He finally came out near a kingdom where he stayed on to tend the king's sheep.

Soon a terrible calamity befell the kingdom. A great dragon crawled out of the churning sea and demanded that the king's three daughters be given to it for its dinner. The dragon said that if its wish were not granted, it would churn up

11

the sea with its tail and great waves would flood the king's cities.

The king was heartbroken. He promised his youngest daughter in marriage to anyone who would slay the dragon. The word was spread far and wide, but no one was brave enough to come forward.

The king bewailed his daughters' fate, but tears and sighs were of no help. The very next morning his elder daughter was to be taken to the dragon for its dinner.

The younger brother heard of this. He could not see why the princess had to end her life in the dragon's belly. All that day he tended the flocks, but during the night he and his faithful animals forged a mighty sword.

At the crack of dawn a palace groom drove the eldest princess to the dragon, passing the meadow where the younger brother was tending the flocks.

"Hey, there! Where are you going?" the shepherd called to the groom.

"To the dragon. Where else would we be going? Are you so brave you'd count the dragon's teeth, shepherd?"

"I might try," the younger brother replied and followed the cart.

The groom pulled up on the sand by the churning sea. The eldest princess stepped down, weeping bitter tears and pleading for someone to come to her rescue. But no, the groom quickly led the horses away from the water's edge and from the trouble, saying that he was unarmed and could not take on the dragon alone.

Then the sea turned dark and terrible and a three-headed monster appeared from the waves.

The younger brother's faithful animals attacked it, while he jumped onto one of the horses and struck off the dragon's three heads with a single blow of his mighty sword. He then cut out their tongues and tossed them into his shepherd's bag. Saying not a word to anyone, as if this were only as it should be, he went quietly back to the flocks.

The groom, meanwhile, wanted to play the hero and said to the princess, "See? We saved you! But mind you don't tell a soul that the shepherd was here, too, or I'll kill you. If the king asks you, you're to say, 'The groom took me to the sea and brought me back again. He's the one to be rewarded.'"

The princess had no choice but to consent, for she did not want to lose her life.

The very next day a six-headed monster appeared from the churning sea.

The same groom now took the king's second daughter to be

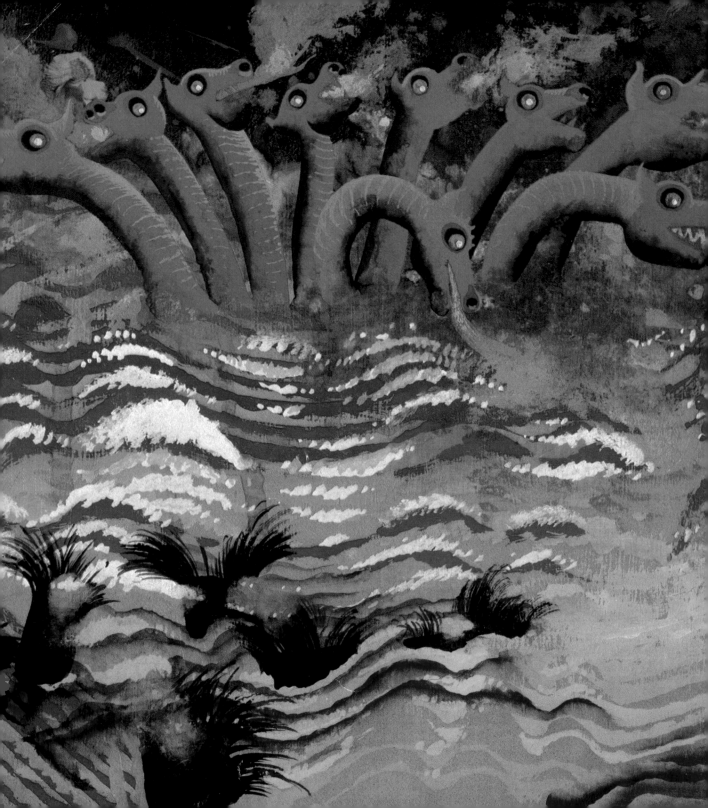

the dragon's dinner, passing the same meadow where the younger brother was tending the flocks. This time, too, the shepherd saved the princess. When he cut off the dragon's six tongues he tossed them into his bag again.

On the third day the same groom took the king's youngest daughter to be the dragon's dinner, for a third time passing the meadow where the younger brother was tending the flocks. And for the third time the shepherd followed the cart.

For a third time the groom stopped the cart on the sand by the churning sea. The youngest princess stepped down, weeping bitter tears and pleading for someone to rescue her. But no, for a third time the groom quickly led the horses away from the water's edge and from trouble, saying that he was unarmed and could not take on the dragon alone.

Then the sea turned dark and terrible and a nine-headed monster appeared from the waves. The younger brother's faithful animals attacked it, while he struck off the dragon's nine heads with a single blow of his mighty sword. At this the youngest princess slipped the shepherd her ring when the groom was not looking. The younger brother bowed low and then cut out the dragon's nine tongues and tossed them into his shepherd's bag. Saying not a word to anyone, as if this were only as it should be, he went quietly back to the flocks.

The groom, meanwhile, wanted to play the hero and said to the princess, "See? We saved you!  But mind you don't tell a soul that the shepherd was here, too, or I'll kill you. If the king asks you, you're to say, 'The groom took me to the sea and brought me back again. He's the one to be rewarded.' "

The youngest princess had no choice but to consent, for she did not want to lose her life.

Meanwhile, the king was overcome with joy. He embraced the groom and said, "You've saved all my daughters from a terrible death. Now hear my will: I give you the youngest princess in marriage and half of my kingdom besides."

No sooner said than done. The wedding was to be held in three days' time.

But what about the shepherd? Well, he shouldered his bag and made his way into the palace.

When the youngest princess saw him she said to her father, "I'll marry the one who has my ring and who rescued me from the dragon."

Just then the groom handed the princess a goblet of wine. She took a sip and passed it on to the shepherd. He,

in turn, dropped her ring into it when the groom was not looking.

Then the princess said to the king, "He is the one who saved me!"

But the king would not believe her.

"If my ring is not proof enough, then I shall marry the one who has the dragons' tongues."

"Come," said the king to the groom, "show us the dragons' tongues, for the wedding feast awaits us."

But where was the groom to get them if he did not have them? There was nothing he could say.

Meanwhile, the younger brother came to stand beside the princess and showed the king all eighteen of the dragons' tongues.

The king said the shepherd was to be dressed in cloth of gold and married to his youngest daughter, while the sly and sneaky groom was to be banished from the palace forever.

Thus did the younger brother marry the beautiful princess and receive half of the kingdom besides. His life was a happy one from that day on.

One day, however, he decided to go to the oak-tree and look at his brother's knife. It was rusted to the very hilt and that meant his brother was in great trouble. Though he hated to part with his wife, the younger brother called to his faithful dog, antelope, wolf and hare and set off to search for his brother.

He walked on and on until he came to a hewn castle with the front and sides made of pine and the turret lost in the clouds. Though there was not a soul outside, a young maiden sat by the window.

"Tell me, pretty maiden, where has everyone gone?" the younger brother said.

"They went off to track the great White Deer, but they've all been turned into grey rocks and stones. Another hunter came by here. He was also looking for the White Deer."

"Why, that was my brother! I must rescue him."

The riddle was short, but the story is longer.

When the younger brother reached the gate he saw the great White Deer running by. He dashed after it with his faithful animals at his heels. But it was not as easy as he thought, for the White Deer simply vanished, with a faint haze to mark the spot where it had been.

An old hag sat by a fire at the edge of the forest nearby. The younger brother went up to her and said, "Tell me, Granny, what are all these grey rocks and stones about here?"

"Just let me pat your beasties first. I shan't harm them," she said. "Then I'll tell you."

"Oh, no. You're as sly as a fox, but I'm no fool, either. See how sharp my sword is?"

And so the old witch had to confess. "These rocks were once people and those stones were animals," she said. "Your brother's one of them."

"Tell me how to break the spell, and don't forget, my sword is very sharp."

"See the fire? Take some ashes from it and sprinkle them over the rocks and stones."

The younger brother did just that. Indeed, the rocks turned into people, a whole kingdom of people, with their king among them. And there was his elder brother and his faithful beasts. The animals all rushed at the witch and that was the end of her.

How happy everyone was! The king gave the elder brother his daughter in marriage, for the witch had cast a spell on her, too, and the princess could never leave the palace until the spell was broken.

The younger brother returned to his wife and they lived happily ever after.

But what about the White Deer?

Listen, and you shall hear. At the very moment the witch

died the White Deer tripped over a tree stump and the spell the witch had cast on it was broken. From then on it ran freely through the forests, never bringing harm to anyone.

# THE SEA BRIDE*

Once upon a time there was a little house on the seashore, and in it lived a poor fisherman. All that his large family had to eat was the fish he caught in the sea.

Then it came to pass that for eight days in a row his nets caught nothing but mud and seaweed. They all went hungry. On the ninth day the fisherman went out to sea with the first rays of the sun. But on this day too his nets did not bring in a single fish. The poor man was in despair. How could he return home empty-handed to his starving children? And the sun was already low in the sky.

Suddenly out of nowhere a boat came sailing towards him. A big one at that, for he could see nine men in it. They called to him:

"Hey, fisherman! Got a good catch?"

*English translation © Raduga Publishers 1986

"I'll say! Not a single fish in nine days," he replied and then froze in horror.

For the boat had sailed closer, and now he could see that instead of nine men in it there was only one—with nine heads.

"And you won't catch another fish until you give me your first-born son to work for me," said the Nine-Headed Monster. "You'll starve to death and your children with you."

The fisherman was so dismayed he could not utter a word.

"Do not fear for your son," said the Nine-Headed Monster. "I shall give him light work, feed him all he desires, and pay him for his labours. And the fish will swim into your nets. I shall wait for you tomorrow at sunset by Big Rock. Do as I say, you will not regret it." So saying he sailed away.

The fisherman returned home and told them everything. They looked at the first-born son, who said:

"Alright, Father, take me to him tomorrow, the Nine-Headed Monster. We can't all starve to death. And I'm not afraid of him anyway."

As the rim of the sun began to rise out of the sea, the fisherman came to Big Rock with his son. The Nine-Headed Monster was already there. He put the lad in his boat and sailed off.

The fisherman gazed after them, but saw nothing, for his eyes were blinded with tears. He had given away his first-born son for a strange monster to take to the ends of the earth. Yet how could he have refused when there was naught to eat.

The Nine-Headed Monster sailed on and on until they saw a mountain towering out to the sea. They sailed up to it. The Nine-Headed Monster got out of the boat and disappeared.

The lad waited and waited for him. The sun rose high in the sky, then began to sink down lower and lower, but still the Nine-Headed Monster did not return.

The lad climbed out of the boat and drew it up onto the shore.

Not knowing where to go, he made his way up to the mountain. In the mountain was a hole. He looked in and something seemed to be shining inside, a long way off.

The lad went through the opening along a passage that grew higher and wider until at last he came to some copper gates. He stopped and gave a light knock on the gates. Not a sound. He knocked a bit louder, but there was still not a sound.

Then he struck the gates with all his might.

They opened, and out came a fair maid.

"Where are you from, bold youth?" she asked.

"I am looking for my master. The Nine-Headed Monster has hired me to work for him. Do you, perchance, know where he is?"

"He is here. He has been fast asleep since morning."

"It was this morning that he brought me here. I have been waiting for him ever since. He went off without saying anything. And now it is nearly night-time..."

"Well, you're a patient one and no mistake. I'll bet you're hungry, eh? Come with me and I'll feed you."

The maid fed him and asked:

"Do you fear the Nine-Headed Monster?"

"No, I do not."

"Do you think you can please him?"

"I do not know. But I shall try."

The maid took a liking to the lad.

"You cannot please the Nine-Headed Monster," she said to him. "But I can help you to outwit and vanquish him, if you do exactly as I say."

"I will do exactly as you say. I am no coward."

"Listen, then. The Nine-Headed Monster will soon awake. He will try to send you off to work, but you must say you only agreed to work in the day. At night your eyes go blind and you cannot see. He will threaten you, but you must stand

31

firm. Do not give way. He will thrash you, but you be patient and keep quiet. Don't utter a single word. Will you stick it out to the bitter end?"

"I will."

"Well, if you do stick it out, I shall tell you what to do next."

Everything happened as the maid had foretold.

The Nine-Headed Monster awoke and tried to send the lad off to work. The lad said he could not see at night. He could only work in the day-time. The Nine-Headed Monster got angry and began to push and threaten him. But the lad remained firm. "I can't see at night. I agreed to work in the day."

Then the Nine-Headed Monster fell upon him and began to thrash him mercilessly.

The lad bore it all in silence.

The Nine-Headed Monster went on thrashing him, but the lad did not utter a sound. He bit his lip and suffered in silence.

At last the Nine-Headed Monster got tired of thrashing the lad, flung him aside and spat angrily. "I didn't hear a sound from you, damn you! Are you made of stone?" Then he spat again and went to sleep.

As soon as the Nine-Headed Monster started snoring, the maid appeared.

"You stuck it out," she said. "Well done!"

But the lad could not move a limb. He just lay where the Nine-Headed Monster had flung him.

The maid knelt by his side and began to rub ointment into his wounds and scratches. Suddenly the lad felt the pain disappear like magic, leaving him bigger and stronger than before. He marvelled at this.

"Do not be surprised," the maid said to him. "The Nine-Headed Monster's strength has flown into you. All the strength that he used up on thrashing you is now yours. So eat and sleep now. You must gain much more strength before you can get the better of the Nine-Headed Monster. Tonight he will thrash you again. But remember: you must not make a sound."

That night the same thing happened. The Nine-Headed Monster told the lad to go to work, but the lad said:

"I agreed to work in the day, master. I can't work at night. I can't see anything."

Hearing this the Nine-Headed Monster began to thrash him with all his might.

The lad gritted his teeth and bore it in silence.

The Nine-Headed Monster thrashed him hard and long. At last he got tired and spat again.

"Still didn't make a sound, damn him!" he said.

Then he cursed and went to bed.

As soon as she heard him snoring, the maid appeared. She healed the lad's wounds with her ointment. And as soon as the pain had gone, he felt twice as strong as yesterday.

But the maid said to him:

"No, you need to be even stronger. You will have to suffer it again."

The third night the Nine-Headed Monster thrashed the lad even harder.

The lad bore it in silence, and just as he thought he could endure it no longer, the Nine-Headed Monster flung him aside. He was at the end of his strength and gnashed his teeth furiously.

"He still hasn't made a sound, curse him!"

The Nine-Headed Monster went off and lay down to sleep.

The maid appeared and with her ointment healed all his wounds, scratches and bruises.

Then the lad said to her:

"I am three times as strong as I was yesterday."

The maid was overjoyed.

"Good," she said. "I have got a sharp sword for you and this ointment. Take the sword and cut off the Monster's nine foul heads. Only hurry. Don't give him time to get his strength back. And remember that if he breathes fire on you, you must pour this ointment on the flames and hack away with all your might. Do not rest or falter until you have cut off all his heads."

The lad seized the sword, rushed off to the Nine-Headed Monster and straightway cut off three of his heads.

The Nine-Headed Monster was so enraged that he began to breathe fire on the lad.

But, slippery as an eel, the lad dodged the flames and poured ointment on them.

They fought like this hard and long, until at last the Nine-Headed Monster began to grow weak. Then the lad summoned up all his strength and cut off the remaining heads one by one.

When the last head fell, the mountain shook, everything collapsed and on the spot where the mountain had stood a splendid city appeared.

Then the maid came up to the lad and said:

"If I am dear to you, be king in this town."

"You are a good and fair maid. I fell in love with you at first sight. But who are you?"

"I am the Sea King's daughter," said the maid. "My father was killed by the Nine-Headed Monster, who put a spell on our kingdom and kept me captive. Now the reign of the

Nine-Headed Monster is ended, and we can celebrate our wedding this very day."

"No," said the lad. "I must invite my relatives to my wedding. And my good friends must dance at it too."

"Be it as you say," the maid agreed. "Invite them all. Here is my ring. Twist it three times around your finger and it will take you wherever you like in a trice. Only be sure not to boast about me, or it will be the worse for you."

The lad put the ring on his finger, twisted it three times and found himself at home. His father and mother were beside themselves with joy! They had given up all hope of ever seeing him alive, and now here he was out of the blue, big and strong and handsome. He told his mother and father all, invited them to the wedding and went to summon his friends and relations.

As he went past a rich man's house, the rich man happened to be walking in his yard. He saw the lad and for want of anything better to do began asking him questions.

"Where have you been all this time? Haven't seen you for ages."

"I sailed off to seek my fortune," the lad replied, eager to be on his way.

"And did you find it?" the rich man continued.

"Yes, I did. I'm going to invite my friends and relations to my wedding."

"And who might the bride be?"

"A good maid."

"And is she pretty?"

"I wouldn't know what to say to that, sir."

"Is she as pretty as my eldest daughter perhaps?"

"Oh, no, sir."

"Then is she perhaps as fair as my second daughter?"

"No, sir."

"Then perhaps she is as beautiful as my youngest daughter?"

At this the lad flew into a rage and said:

"Stop going on at me about your daughters, sir. They're not a patch on my bride. She's a thousand times fairer than they! "

No sooner were the words out of his mouth than the ring disappeared.

He went on his way, weeping bitterly.

How was he to get back to his bride now? How could he find her?

Trudging along the road towards him came an old woman, bent almost double under the weight of the bundle of firewood on her back.

The lad took pity on her.

"Let me give you a hand, granny," he said, taking the bundle from her shoulder.

Now she was no ordinary old woman, but Old Mother Laima herself, who brings good folk happiness.

Old Mother Laima stopped and asked:

"Why are you crying, my son?"

The lad told her everything.

Then Old Mother Laima said to him:

"Why didn't you listen to your bride? She gave you some good advice."

"But I wasn't boasting, granny. I lost my temper, that's why I said it. I didn't like him talking about my bride like that."

"Very well, then. Take this shoe, put it on and go to the Moon. Ask her the way to the enchanted mountain-city."

Only then did the lad realize how fortunate he had been.

He hurried to the Moon and asked her the way. But the Moon said:

"I only go out at night. I don't know the way. You'd better ask the Sun."

The lad hurried to the Sun and said:

"Please show me the way to the enchanted mountain-city. My bride is waiting for me there. Please help me."

"I don't know the way," said the Sun. "Go and ask the Father of the Winds. Perhaps he can help you. The winds fly everywhere. They know every nook and cranny."

So he hurried off to the Father of the Winds and asked him the way.

The Father of the Winds listened to his story, then picked up twelve reed-pipes and blew them. Eleven winds raced up at once, all except the twelfth wind—the north wind.

Then the Father of the Winds blew once more, so loudly that the mountains shook and the trees bowed to the ground.

Some time passed. The Father of the Winds was about to blow again and had lifted the pipe to his lips, when Ziemelis, the north wind, came racing up.

"Why were you such a long time?"

"Sorry, Father. What do you want? I was far away by the enchanted mountain."

"That's exactly what I want. Show this lad the way there."

"But he'd never keep up with me, Father! "

"Don't talk rubbish. He's wearing Old Mother Laima's magic shoe."

So off flew Ziemelis with the lad following him. He kept up all the way, even stepping on the wind's heels, and they reached the enchanted mountain in a trice.

When the lad saw his beautiful Sea Princess he was beside himself with joy.

He married her that very day and they are still living together happily.

But he has never boasted again, not even in a fit of temper.

# ESTONIAN FOLK TALES

## The King of the Mushrooms
Retold by *Matthias Aisan*
Translated by *Irina Zheleznova*
Illustrations by *Jaan Tammsaar*

## The Forbidden Knot
Retold by *Zoya Zadunaiskaya*
Translated by *Kathleen Cook*
Illustrations by *Jaan Tammsaar*

# THE KING OF THE MUSHROOMS*

Once upon a time some men out hunting for mushrooms in the forest found one that was bigger than any they had ever seen before. They began pulling it out of the ground, and lo! —a little old man sprang out from under it. No larger than a finger he was and had a beard that trailed over the ground. The little old man rushed away but the men ran after him. They caught him and asked who he was.

"I am king of all the mushrooms growing in this forest," said the little old man.

The men did not know what to do. They thought and they thought and could think of nothing better than to give the little old man for a gift to their king. This they did and the king rewarded them generously and ordered the little old man to be locked up in the cellar. "I shall hold a big feast," said the king to himself, "and show my guests what funny little bearded old men live under the mushrooms in my forest. Meanwhile, he must stay under lock and key."

Now, the king had a young son. One day the boy was in the courtyard playing with a golden egg and he happened to send it rolling through a window straight into the cellar. The little old man saw the egg and snatched it up.

"Give me back my egg! " the boy called to him.

But the little old man called back:

"I won't! Come and get it yourself."

"How can I do that? The door is locked," the boy said.

"That's nothing. The keys are in the palace. Go and fetch them."

The boy did as he was told, and when he had brought the keys, unlocked the door and came down into the cellar. The little old man gave him the golden egg and himself whisked between the young prince's legs and out of the door and vanished.

The prince, who had not noticed this, now decided to take a good look at the little old man before locking him up again. He gazed round him, and finding the little old man gone, was badly frightened. Locking the door quickly, he took the keys back to the palace and never breathed a word about what had happened to anyone.

The day of the feast arrived and there were many people from all parts of the kingdom who came to attend it. A big crowd gathered round the palace, for everyone had heard that the king had a surprise in store for his guests.

The king now sent a servant of his to fetch the little old man. The servant returned empty-handed, but when he said that the little old man was not in the cellar, the king refused to believe him and himself climbed down into it.

However, what isn't there, isn't there, and though the king felt ashamed at having called together his guests for nothing, he could not conceal from them that the little old man had vanished. He told them that he had got out of the cellar through a mouse-hole, and this they all believed and were very sorry indeed not to have seen him.

Many years passed, and the young prince grew to manhood. Once at dinner the talk turned on the little old man, and the prince confessed that he had sent his golden egg rolling into the cellar and that that was how the little old man had managed to escape.

The king was very angry. He would not listen to anyone, not even to the queen, and drove the prince out of the palace. But he ordered a general to go along with him for company, for he knew that it was easier for two people to roam the world together and take care of themselves.

The prince and the general set off on their way, they walked and they walked and they came to a forest. It was very hot, and the prince felt thirsty, but where were they to get water? They walked on a little further, and there before them was a deep well.

Said the general:

"I'll let you down into the well on a rope if you like, and when you have drunk your fill, I'll pull you out again."

To this the prince agreed, and the general let him down into the well, but when he had drunk his fill, he did not pull him out as he had promised.

"I'll pull you out again on one condition—that from now on you will be the general and I will be the prince," he cried.

What was the prince to do? If he refused, the general would leave him in the well. There was nothing for it but to agree.

The general pulled the prince out of the well and they went on again.

They came to the king of a strange kingdom and asked him if he would take them into his service. And all the time they did as they had agreed, the general calling himself a prince and the prince calling himself a general.

The king invited the sham prince to live in the palace with

him and he made the real one his chief groom. The grooms drove the horses to pasture, and the prince went with them, for it was his job to watch over them.

They came to the forest, the prince sat down on a rock, he thought of his sad plight, and the tears poured from his eyes. All of a sudden who should be there before him but the little old man who he had let out of the cellar all those many years ago.

"Why so sad?" asked the little old man.

"There is no reason for me to be happy," said the prince. "My father drove me out of the palace for having let you escape and now the general has taken over my title. He tells everyone that he is a prince, and I am forced to pasture horses."

"Don't you grieve, everything will turn out for the best," the little old man said. "Come with me to my eldest daughter's palace."

Now, this made the prince very curious.

"Who are you, then?" he asked.

"I am the King of the Mushrooms," said the little old man.

And he led the prince to his eldest daughter's palace. The palace and everything in it was made of copper, and it was truly a place to fill one with wonder! So happy did the prince feel there that he did not notice how the hours passed.

"It is time for you to leave us," said the King of the Mushrooms, "but, as is our custom, we will give you a farewell gift. Ho there! Bring in a copper horse!"

A copper horse was led in, and so spirited was he that it took four men to hold him.

"This is my present to you," said the King of the Mushrooms.

The prince was frightened.

"What will I do with him? Why, it takes four men to hold him!" he said.

"Here are four bottles of my magic potion. Drink it if you want to be strong!" said the King of the Mushrooms.

The prince drank the potion and at once felt so strong that he feared the copper horse no longer.

The King of the Mushrooms brought out a copper pipe.

"Here is a pipe for you," he said. "Take good care of it. If you lose it you will lose your horse as well. And now put on the copper armour that is under the saddle."

The prince put on the armour, sprang on the copper horse's back and rode off at a gallop.

On the following day he went to the forest again to graze the horses, and lo! —there was the King of the Mushrooms before him.

"You will have to pay my middle daughter a visit today," said he.

The prince sprang on the copper horse's back and made off at a gallop for the middle daughter's palace. Now, the middle daughter's palace was a silver one and everything in it was of silver. The time passed quickly, and the King of the Mushrooms had a silver horse brought in and given to the prince as a farewell gift. Eight men held the horse and it was almost more than they could do, so the prince felt that he could not cope with him.

The King of the Mushrooms told the prince to drink eight bottles of his magic potion and to take the silver armour from under the saddle. This the prince did, and he put the armour which sparkled and shone, so well was it furbished. And now the King of the Mushrooms brought out a silver pipe from his pocket.

"Take good care of it or you'll lose your horse," said he.

On the third day the prince went to visit the youngest daughter of the King of the Mushrooms who lived in a palace of gold. There the King of the Mushrooms gave him a golden horse for a present, and as it took twelve men to hold him, the prince had to drink twelve bottles of the magic potion before he grew strong enough to cope with him. The King of

59

the Mushrooms then gave him a golden pipe, and turning to his daughter, said:

"You too must give our guest something."

The youngest daughter brought a golden egg and gave it to the prince, who thanked her, got on his golden horse and galloped away.

He came back to his grooms and on the following day went to see the king in whose service he was. And as he came toward the palace, he met the king's youngest daughter who was weeping loudly.

"What has happened? Why are you crying?" the prince asked.

"How can I help it! " the princess said. "Tomorrow a dragon is going to crawl out of the sea and eat me up. If they don't give me to him he will raze the whole kingdom to the ground."

The prince took pity on the princess. On the following day, when the king's soldiers had lined up by the side of the sea and the princess arrived and stood waiting for the dragon, he went to the forest and blew upon his copper pipe. At once the copper horse appeared before him, and the prince put on his copper armour, sprang on the horse's back and made off at a gallop for the sea.

Meanwhile the dragon had crawled out of the sea on his

four paws, and seeing the people gathered on the shore, gave out a bellow of laughter.

"Is there anyone among you brave enough to fight me?" he asked.

No one replied, and they all stood there in silence when who should come riding up to them on his copper horse but the prince!

"Who are you going to fight for?" asked the dragon.

"For the princess and for myself," the prince replied.

"How are you going to fight—on horseback or on foot?" asked the dragon again.

"On horseback," the prince said. "After all, you have four legs, too, like my horse."

The dragon decided to use cunning. He moved away at first, but then turned round very suddenly and came running back, thinking to swallow the prince together with his horse.

But this was not to be! The prince came at him, smote off his head with a single wave of his sword, threw his body into the sea and galloped off to the forest. But not a word did he say to his grooms, just as if nothing had happened.

On the following day the prince went to see the king again, and there, coming out of the palace and weeping loudly was the king's youngest daughter.

"What has happened?" asked the prince. "Why are you crying?"

"Tomorrow a six-headed dragon is going to crawl out of the sea and eat up my middle sister," the princess said. "How I wish I could find the brave man who saved me, for I know he would save my sister too! "

The prince went back to the forest, and on the following morning he blew upon his silver pipe, and at once the silver horse appeared before him. The prince put on his silver armour, sprang on the horse's back and galloped away. He rode up to the sea and waited for the six-headed dragon to appear.

All of a sudden the sea boiled up, and the six-headed dragon crawled out of the water and challenged the bravest among the men gathered there to battle. But they all ran away and only the prince on his silver horse made straight for him.

"That's right, my son, come closer! " called the dragon. "It will be all the better for me, for I will eat up both you and your horse! "

And the dragon opened wide his jaws.

But the prince's sword flashed, and all of the dragon's six heads rolled down on to the sand like ordinary heads of cabbage.

The prince went back to the forest just as if nothing had

happened, let his silver horse go free and lay down for a sleep.

On the following day he went to see the king, and as he was coming toward the palace, met the princess who was in tears again.

"What has happened?" asked the prince.

"Tomorrow a twelve-headed dragon is going to crawl out of the sea and eat up my eldest sister," the princess said. "How I wish I could find the brave man who saved me and my middle sister!"

The prince took pity on the princess, and when morning came he blew upon his golden pipe. The golden horse appeared before him, and the prince put on his golden armour, sprang on the horse's back and made off at a gallop for the sea.

The eldest princess was already on the shore waiting for the twelve-headed dragon, and the king, his men beside him, was there too, for he wanted to see how his daughter would fare.

After a time there came the most fearful noise, the sea began to seethe and to boil, and the twelve-headed dragon thrust all his twelve heads out of the water and then crawled out all of him on to the shore. The king's men ran away in fright, the king took to his heels, and only the prince on his golden horse made straight for the dragon. The dragon saw him and began to mock and to jeer at him.

"That's right, my son, come closer!" he cried. "It will be all the better for me, for I will eat up both you and your horse!"

And thinking to swallow the prince, he opened wide his jaws. But the prince waved his sword, and six of the dragon's heads rolled to the ground like ordinary heads of cabbage. At this the dragon flew into a rage and began thrashing the prince and his horse with his tail. Smoke poured from the dragon's mouth and steam from his nostrils, and he was about to swallow the prince when the prince looked back and saw the King of the Mushrooms standing there beside a large rock.

"Make haste and crack the golden egg!" said he to the prince.

The prince took the golden egg from his pocket and broke it in two, and at once a whole host of warriors poured out of it and attacked the dragon.

The dragon stood gaping at them, and the prince made good use of this and with one stroke of his sword smote off his six remaining heads. The dragon dropped dead, the prince took out the golden egg, broken though it was, and all the warriors poured back into it.

The dead dragon was left on the beach, and the prince galloped off to the forest and slept there for three days and

three nights on end just as if nothing had happened. On the fourth day he felt someone shaking him, and when he opened his eyes, he saw the King of the Mushrooms standing beside him.

"Get up quickly and go to the king," said the King of the Mushrooms. "That knave of a general of yours is in the palace, demanding that the princess be given him in marriage. He says that it was he who killed the three dragons."

The prince jumped up and blew upon his copper pipe, the copper horse appeared, and the prince put on his copper armour and made off at a gallop for the palace. And he was there just in time to hear the general boasting about how he had vanquished the three dragons. The king's youngest daughter saw the prince and was overjoyed.

"Look, Father, there is the man who saved me!" she cried.

But the prince turned his copper horse round and rode off to the forest. There he blew upon his silver pipe, got off the copper horse and on the silver one and rode back again to the king's palace.

"Look, Father, there is the man who saved me!" the king's middle daughter cried.

But the prince turned round his horse and rode back to the forest. There he blew upon his golden pipe, and getting off his silver horse and on the golden one, made for the king's palace again.

"Look, Father, there is the man who saved me!" the king's eldest daughter cried.

The prince was about to ride back to the forest again, but the king stopped him and said that he wanted to reward him for having saved his daughters.

"There is a prince from a faraway land here who says that he saved my daughters," said the king. "I don't know why they all insist that you were the one who did it."

"The man who is passing himself off as a prince is only a general of mine," the prince said.

The king was much surprised.

"Then you are the prince?" said he. "Well, then, you shall be richly rewarded for your bravery. And you can marry one of my daughters besides. Just choose the one you like best."

But the prince rode off to the forest without waiting for his reward, and the king came back to the palace and drove out the general.

The prince now made straight for the golden palace where lived the youngest daughter of the King of the Mushrooms, she who had given him the golden egg. They were married then and there and lived together happily ever after. But as for the King of the Mushrooms, from that day on no one laid eyes on him again.

# THE FORBIDDEN KNOT*

It was a bad year for the fishing village. The catches had been poor ever since autumn, and by spring the larders were empty. Fish is to the fisherman what grain is to the peasant. When there is no fish, the whole village goes hungry.

The fishermen gathered together and racked their brains. What could they do? It was too early in the year to go out to sea, but to stay at home would mean certain ruin.

So they thought and thought, then resolved to try their luck.

"Perhaps the sea will take pity on us and send something into our nets at least!"

Then one fisherman said:

"I don't know whether it's true, but they say Old Man Kaarel used to be friendly with the Sea Queen herself. He

*English translation ©Raduga Publishers 1986

must know how to get a good catch."

"I seem to remember something about that too," said a second. "I was still a boy when my grandfather said that Kaarel had some special thing that lured the fish at all seasons. Why don't we go and see the old man. Perhaps he'll give us it to try our luck."

Old Man Kaarel's house was right on the edge of the village. He had once been a brave and successful fisherman. But time had long since bent his back, and now he had not only stopped going out to sea, but rarely crossed the threshold of his little house. Yet when the fishermen knocked on his door, Kaarel went out to them and said:

"I know why you have come to me, friends, and this is what I have to say: a good fisherman relies on his skill and the strength of his hands, not on good luck. But you have taken on a hard task. You are going out to sea before the season, and the sea does not like that. Never mind, go ahead bravely, and I will help you."

So saying Old Man Kaarel took the kerchief from his neck and showed it to the fishermen.

"See the three knots in this kerchief. The first will bring you a fair wind. Undo it as you hoist the sail. The second will draw the fish into your nets. Undo it as you cast them. And the third must never be undone. Woe betide you if you do. And one another thing. Be content with what the sea sends you. Whatever your catch, do not cast your nets a second time."

"Don't worry, Kaarel," replied the fishermen. "We'll do just as you say. We give you our word."

"Remember that a seaman's word must never be broken," the old man said, handing the fishermen his kerchief.

All night long the fishermen pitched their boat and mended their nets. By morning all was ready.

The fishermen jumped into the boat and pushed off.

They were soon out of the gulf and hoisted the sail. The captain pulled out Old Man Kaarel's kerchief and said:

"Let's undo the first knot."

They undid the first knot. At once a fresh wind blew up, filled the sails and sent the boat racing along.

It sailed splendidly, turning without the rudder and cutting the waves like a knife. The fishermen sailed far out into the open sea. Suddenly the wind dropped, the sail went limp and the boat stopped.

"This must be the place the old man was talking about," said the fishermen. "Let's cast our nets here."

So they all set to work. They lay anchor, spread out the nets and cast them into the sea.

"Now undo the second knot!" cried the fishermen.

The captain took Old Man Kaarel's kerchief out of his jacket and undid the knot. No sooner had he undone it, than there was a great rippling and splashing in the sea that made the floats on the nets bob wildly.

The fishermen waited until everything had calmed down, then cautiously began to pull in their nets. Never before had they been so heavy. The fishermen had to pull with all their might. At last the edge of the nets appeared above the water. They were teeming with fish. The silver scales glittering so brightly in the sun dazzled their eyes.

"Heave ho, my lads!" the captain ordered.

The fishermen tugged at the nets and the fish tumbled into the boat.

"It's a fine catch!" said one of the fishermen. "Thanks to Old Man Kaarel."

"That's as may be," replied another fisherman. "But to last all of us until the start of the fishing season, we need three catches like that. Shouldn't we cast the nets again, friends?"

"What are you saying?" exclaimed the youngest fisherman. "Remember what Old Man Kaarel told us: be content with what the sea sends you."

"Ah, the needs of the old and young are small indeed,"

laughed the captain. "But we'd be ashamed to go home with a boat that's not full to the brim."

So the fishermen cast their nets again.

But this time they were not so lucky. The nets they hauled in were empty. They hadn't caught a single fish.

The fishermen's spirits fell, but the captain said:

"That's because we haven't undone the third knot in Old Man Kaarel's kerchief. It's no ordinary kerchief, as you yourselves can see. Each knot brings success. There is one left, so we will undo that too. Then our boat will be full up."

"But, captain," the oldest fisherman now spoke up. "Old Man Kaarel told us not to touch that knot."

"You're an old man yourself," replied the captain. "And old men have a well-known saying—don't try your luck a third time. But there's another saying too—only a fool turns down good fortune."

"That's for sure," said the fishermen. "Let's give it a try then! Undo the knot, captain."

The captain had been holding the kerchief ready for some time. He tugged at the knot and undid it. The sea roared, the waves rose up over the stern, and the floats on the nets danced madly.

"There go the fish!" said the captain. "I told you so!"

The fishermen were so overjoyed they could hardly wait until it was time to haul in the nets. Again, like the first time, the nets seemed very heavy. But fishermen are a strong breed. They hauled the ropes together hard and pulled out the net. But wait a minute! What was that! There was only one fish in the net. A huge pike with a blunt tail, as if the end had been chopped off with an axe.

"Did you ever see the likes of that!" exclaimed the fishermen, flinging the pike angrily into the boat.

Meanwhile the sun was sinking low on the horizon. The sea grew calmer with the approach of sunset.

Suddenly some voices drifted over the quiet water. The fishermen jumped up and looked about them.

"Who else has hunger driven out to sea?" they wondered.

But there was no sign of a boat anywhere.

"It must have been a seagull," the captain said.

Then they heard the long, vibrant sound of a horn, like someone calling the cows in the village. And a woman's voice asked:

"Everyone awake? Everyone at home?"

"Yes, everyone except that fool without a tail," replied a young girl's sweet voice.

Then the horn sounded again, even louder and longer.

Suddenly the pike in the boat began to thresh about.

It opened its sharp-toothed mouth wide and jostled the other fish with all its might. But the captain kicked it and shouted loudly to the crew:

"Raise anchor! I don't like the look of this. Let's be off as fast as we can."

The fishermen raised the anchor and turned the boat towards their native shore.

But what was this! No matter how hard they plied the oars, the boat would not budge. As if the sea had frozen or the boat become rooted to the seabed. They pulled hard together, but it did not move an inch.

All night long the fishermen laboured, flinging down the oars in despair, then picking them up again to have another try, but to no avail. It seemed that nothing on earth could move the boat.

When the first flush of dawn appeared in the east they heard the strange voices again.

"Everyone awake? Everyone at home?"

"Everyone's awake and at home except that fool without a tail. There's still no sign of him."

Then came the sound of the horn again and the tinkling of little bells. Suddenly the fish in the boat stirred. Opening its sharp-toothed mouth and moving its gills, it began to wriggle up the side of the boat.

"What's that monster up to now?" muttered the captain. Suddenly he thought: "Perhaps that's who they're waiting for."

The captain jumped up, grabbed the pike and threw it overboard.

At that very moment someone far away, perhaps on the seabed, clapped their hands and cried happily:

"Look, look! That fool without a tail is swimming home. In such a hurry that he's blowing bubbles!"

The fishermen heard no more. A terrible wind arose and the waves roared so loud that the fishermen could not even hear one another.

The boat was swept away by the waves.

All day the fishermen were tossed about in the raging sea. The boat would fly up as if to the clouds, then plunge down, down to the very depths. The old men could not remember such a storm in all their days.

Towards evening they reached a rocky island. The fishermen jumped ashore and dragged the boat onto dry land.

"What island is this?" they asked one another. "Where has the storm taken us?"

At that very moment a little old man appeared from behind a cliff. His back was bent almost double, and his white beard all but touched the ground.

"This is the island of Hiu-maa," said the old man. "Small wonder that you don't know it. Men rarely put to shore here of their own free will."

The old man led the fishermen to a wooden hut behind the cliffs, where he warmed and fed them, then asked:

"Who are you and where are you from, and why are you fishing so early?"

"What else could we do! Our larders are empty, there is naught to eat in the village," the fishermen replied and told the old man all that had happened. One thing only did they keep back—how they had undone the third, forbidden, knot on Old Man Kaarel's kerchief.

The old man listened to them and said:

"I used to know that Kaarel of yours. Do you know where he sent your boat? To the pastures of the Sea Queen, where she takes her fish. But her fish are clever, they would never get caught. The shoals of fish you caught had come from far away to feed with the shoals of the Sea Queen. But how that tailless pike swam into your nets, I can't understand. How did you manage to catch it?"

Then the fishermen realized what Kaarel had tried to protect them against, but they said nothing to the old man. Their spirits were low. The storm was still raging at sea, the wind howled down the chimney, and heavy spray splashed against the window. The bad weather was here to stay.

The old man put the fishermen to bed on some old nets in a corner of the hut, and they slept soundly.

At dawn the old man woke them up. Outside the storm was still raging, and the waves were dashing against the cliffs. The fishermen's hearts were heavy.

"What are we to do?" they asked the old man. "We'll never be able to leave here, and our hungry children are waiting for us at home."

"Never fear," the old man replied. "Perhaps you will be able to get away. Give me Old Man Kaarel's kerchief."

The captain took out the kerchief reluctantly and handed it to the old man.

The old man looked at the kerchief and shook his head.

"I've seen this once before. Only I seem to remember there were three knots in it. You undid two of them, you told me so yourselves, but where is the third?"

What were the fishermen to do? They told the old man the whole truth.

The old man frowned.

"You are bad fishermen!" he said. "You disobeyed Old Man Kaarel and you tried to deceive me."

The fishermen hung their heads in shame.

"Well," the old man said. "I can see you have been punished already. For the sake of Old Man Kaarel and your starving children, I will help you."

Then the old man took the kerchief, tied a knot in it and said:

"Make sure that from now on your word is kept as firmly as this knot."

As soon as he drew the knot tight, the wind dropped and the waves grew calm, as if there had never been a storm.

The fishermen thanked the old man and set off for their boat.

The old man went with them to the seashore. As they hoisted the sail, he waved his hand in farewell. And straightway a light breeze filled the sail and sent the boat racing over the calm sea.

The fishermen reached home the very same day.

They were greeted joyfully by their friends and families.

And their catch lasted until the beginning of the season.

So all's well that ends well. But the fishermen never forgot the lesson they had been taught. Ever since then a

seaman's word has been kept as firmly as the knots he ties in his ropes.

And you would do well to remember this story too. For it is not only seamen who should keep their word.

# LITHUANIAN FOLK TALE

## The Sun Princess and the Prince

Retold by *Aldona Liobyte* and *Jurgis Dovydajtis*
Translated by *Irina Zheleznova*
Illustrations by *Vanga Gedmantaite-Galkuviene*

# THE SUN PRINCESS AND THE PRINCE*

Long, long ago, beyond the nine mountains and the nine forests, there lived a king and a queen. A son was born to them, and they loved him to distraction. When he grew up, the prince had plenty of puffs and cream to eat, and he wore clothing spun of silver and gold. At his bidding, as if out of thin air, servants in braided coats and grooms in bright caftans appeared, and snow-white wolfhounds followed him about and never took their eyes off him. And as for his father and mother, they would have caught the sun itself in a sieve and brought it to him if only they could. But the young prince was always gloomy. He would send away his servants and chase away his dogs, walk sadly about in the palace garden and complain of his lot.

"I have no sister and no brother, no one to play with, no

one to talk to. Why is that, Mother?" he asked. "Tell me."

To this the queen would make no reply but only drop her eyes, and clapping her hands, order the court ladies to play their golden cymbals and amuse the prince. But the prince's heart was heavy, and nothing could cheer him.

Now, near the palace was a courtyard surrounded by a high stone wall. The wall was gilded and had razor-sharp diamond spikes on it, and if anyone tried to climb it he was in danger of being pierced through. The prince was warned never so much as to come near the wall, but this only made him all the more eager to learn what there was behind it. But though he kept asking the queen and the courtiers about it, they would tell him nothing.

One day a raven perched on the top of the wall. Seeing him the prince took his bow and was about to shoot his arrow when the raven said in a human voice:

"Spare me, Prince, and I will tell you a secret. Behind this wall is a garden where grow many roses and lilies, and in the garden is a palace where your three sisters are kept under lock and key. If you want to see them, look for a little golden key which lies under a flowerpot in the queen's chamber. And remember this: once you are in the garden, open the window of your sisters' chamber and let them breathe some fresh air."

The raven flapped his wings and flew away, and the prince

stood there as if frozen to the spot, not knowing whether or not it had all been a dream.

That night, when everyone was asleep, he rose quietly, fondled his dogs to keep them from barking, and stealing into the queen's chamber, found the flowerpot and, under it, the golden key.

He felt along the wall in the darkness, discovered a secret door, unlocked it, went into the garden and opened the window of his sisters' chamber. And his three sisters kissed him and thanked him again and again for letting them breathe the fresh air, smell the flowers and admire the beauty of the stars.

All of a sudden the earth quaked and trembled, and a black column of dust rose up into the air like smoke from a chimney. The three sisters were caught up by a whirlwind and swept out of the window. The prince, who feared that he was to blame for this, began to weep, to call his dear sisters and to curse himself for his foolish curiosity. But his tears did not help. The sisters were gone, their chamber was empty, and only the stars twinkled overhead as before.

Morning came, and the queen rose and prepared to take some food to her daughters. She looked for the key, but it was gone. She ran to the palace where her daughters were kept, but there was no one there!

"My poor daughters! I will never see them again!" the queen

cried, wringing her hands. "The dragon must have eaten them!"

Learning of his daughters' disappearance, the king flew into a temper. He raged and stormed, his voice rang like thunder in the palace and his courtiers shook with fear. Some of them hid themselves in their rooms, others brought out their crystal balls and gazed into them to see what the future held, but none could say who had let out the princesses or where to seek them.

Learning that innocent people were being herded to the palace, the prince went to see the king.

"It is I who am to blame for what happened to my sisters, Father, so you must punish *me* for it," he said.

At this the king's face grew darker than a storm cloud.

"Before you were born the wise men who read the stars warned me that your sisters would be carried off by a dragon," said he. "That was why I built that wall and kept them under lock and key. But you disobeyed me and defied my orders. So, worthless youth that you are, leave my kingdom and do not return until you have brought back your sisters."

And the king opened the gate of the palace with his own hands and told the prince to go where he would. The queen burst into tears, but she only managed to embrace her son and to thrust some pies in his hands before the gate shut behind him.

Not knowing what to do or where to go, the prince set off

along the road. On and on he walked over hills and dales, across fields and meadows, and when night came he climbed a tree and tied himself to it so as not to fall off it in his sleep and be eaten up by some wild animal.

He journeyed thus for many days, following many roads and trails, till he came to a strange land. Footsore and weary, he stopped by a hut, knocked at the door and asked to be let in for the night. An old woman came out, and standing on the threshold, asked him where he was going. The prince told her about his sisters, and the old woman said:

"You won't find them soon, my lad. The way that lies before you is far and dangerous, and you are timid of heart and unused to work. Stay with me for three years, learn to earn your own living, and then I may be able to help you."

The prince stayed with the old woman. He uprooted trees, ploughed fields, ground grain and made shoes of bast. It was hard work, all of it, but so strong was his wish to save his sisters that he would not give up.

Three years flew by, and the old woman called the prince to her side.

"Tomorrow you can set out to seek your sisters," said she. "Here is a ball of yarn for you. Wherever it rolls, there you must go. And here is a piece of bread. Whenever you are hungry, eat of it, it will last you a long time."

The prince took leave of the old woman and set off on his journey again. The ball of yarn rolled ahead of him and showed him the way, the piece of bread in his bag grew no smaller no matter how much of it he ate, the streams and brooks gave him water to drink, and the birds cheered him with their songs.

By and by he came to a copper mountain on which grew a copper forest. He climbed a tree and began trying to break off a branch to make a staff for himself when all of a sudden, as if out of thin air, a four-eyed witch came flying up to him, making a great racket as she flew.

"Who is breaking off branches in my forest?" she cried.

The prince threw his ball of yarn at her, and she rushed to catch it and knocked her head against a tree. And as she stood there swaying on her feet and trying to get back her breath, the prince climbed the copper mountain. On its top was a copper palace, and sitting at a spinning wheel by one of the palace windows, was his elder sister. She recognized her brother at once, welcomed him lovingly and gave him many nice things to eat. But when evening came she began to fret and to worry and she hid the prince in a beautifully ornamented chest behind a curtain.

The trees in the forest hummed and droned, the copper leaves rang and jangled, and a falcon came flying up. He cast off his feathers at the door and turned into a tall and hand-

some young man. Seeing the branch the prince had lopped off, he asked his wife, the prince's sister, who had dared to touch his tree. She would tell him nothing at first, but then said:

"What would you do, Falcon, if my brother came to pay me a visit?"

"Would be glad to see him and would thank him for delivering you from captivity."

The sister called the prince, who came out from his hiding place, and Falcon welcomed him warmly and told him that he had been put under a spell by an evil sorceress and was fated to be a falcon for six more years, that only the Sun Princess could break the spell and that he had not been able to find her though he flew round the earth three times every day.

"I will find her for you," the prince said.

"You'll only be killed, my brother," said his sister. "Many brave men tried to get into the palace of the Sun Princess, but none of them ever came back."

But the prince would not listen to her, and Falcon gave him a kerchief as a parting gift and said:

"If ever you are in trouble, take out this kerchief and you shall see what you shall see."

The prince thanked Falcon, but though he felt very much at home in his sister's house, he longed to be off and on his way to see his other sisters. So he bade Falcon and his wife goodbye, and hiding the kerchief in his bosom, set off again after the old woman's ball of yarn.

By and by he came to a silver mountain on which grew a silver forest. He began breaking off a silver branch to make a staff for himself when all of a sudden, as if out of thin air, two witches who were guarding the forest came flying up to him, whistling as they flew. The prince threw his ball of yarn at them, and they rushed to catch it, bumped against each other and fell to the ground. The prince at once climbed the silver mountain and came to a silver palace, and there, sitting at one of the palace windows and working on a piece of embroidery, was his middle sister. The prince stepped inside and found himself in a silver chamber with windows of crystal and floors of marble. He told his sister who he was, but she would not believe him at first and only did when she heard of his journey and of their elder sister's copper palace. She then set food and drink before him and chattered away happily, but after a while she became sad and woebegone.

"It's a pity you can't stay with me longer, brother," she said, "but Bear, my husband, might come and claw you to death."

"Don't be afraid, sister, I'll hide from him," said the prince.

Evening arrived, the earth began to quake and to tremble, the silver trees to creak and to moan, and there was a bear at the door. He came inside, cast off his skin and turned into a tall and handsome young man. Seeing the silver staff, he asked his wife, whose it was.

"My brother's," the wife said. "He paid me a visit and left his staff here."

"Why didn't he wait for me to come back?"

"I was afraid you would claw him to death, so I told him to go away. But never you mind, for I think I can catch him up."

She went out onto the porch and called the prince, who at once came out of his hiding place. He and Bear greeted each other, and Bear said that an evil magician had put a spell on him, that every day on the stroke of midnight he turned into a bear and that he would remain under the spell for four more years unless the Sun Princess came to his aid.

"I will go to the Sun Princess and ask her to help you," said the prince.

"It won't be easy, but there's no harm in trying," said Bear. "And I, for my part, will do what I can for you. Here is a pot of porridge. You have only to put some of it wherever you like and anyone who touches it will be stuck fast to it."

The prince bade his middle sister and Bear, her husband, goodbye, and set off on his way again to seek his youngest sister.

The ball of yarn rolled over hills and dales, it rolled across fields and forests, and it reached the seashore. There was an island in the middle of the sea, and on the island was a golden palace. Sea monsters thrust their heads up out of the water and gnashed their teeth, but this did not daunt the prince who jumped into the waves after the ball of yarn and swam to the island. He reached it soon enough and found himself in a golden forest. But the ground under the trees was boggy, and hiding there were hideous-looking witches. The prince climbed one of the trees and smeared some of his magic porridge over its trunk, and smelling the porridge, the witches rushed to the tree. They sniffed at it, trying to find out who was sitting on its top, and at once got their noses stuck to the trunk. Now there was no one to stop the prince from making his way to the golden palace or going inside it.

The first chamber he came to was empty and so was the second chamber, and it was only in the third chamber that he found his youngest sister. She sat there rolling a golden apple about on a plate, and oh, how pleased she and the prince were to see each other again! They began talking, and the hours passed very quickly, but after a while the sister's face clouded.

"Pike, my husband, will be back soon," she said, "and he might eat you up."

Seeing how worried she was, the prince promised his sister not to show himself to his brother-in-law and hid in one of the chambers.

All of a sudden the palace quaked and trembled, great waves

struck the windows, and a huge pike leapt up out of the water. He cast off his scales at the door, turned into a tall and handsome young man and asked his wife who it was that had been to see them. Learning that it was the prince, her brother, he began to scold her for having let him leave so soon.

The wife then called to the prince, who at once came out of his hiding place. They sat down at the table, and, oh, what nice things they had to eat!

But their good spirits did not last long. Pike grew sad and crestfallen, and he said to the prince:

"I'm sorry, my brother, but you and I must now part. It is almost midnight, and I will lose my proper shape on the stroke of it and turn into a pike again. An evil witch cast this spell on me, and it will not be broken for three more years unless the Sun Princess comes to my aid."

"I will go to see the Sun Princess and beg her to help you and my other brothers-in-law!" the prince said.

"No one who went to see the Sun Princess ever came back again," said Pike. "But I won't try to stop you. Here is a golden casket for you. Open it if ever you are in trouble."

The prince took the casket and set off again after the ball of yarn to seek the kingdom of the Sun Princess.

Whether a long time passed or a short, nobody knows, but he came to the Sun Princess's kingdom and found her palace. On

either side of the gate was a pillar of fire, and when anyone came near them, the pillars would draw together and burn him to death.

The prince threw down his ball of yarn and sent it rolling ahead of him, the pillars drew together, and lo!—only a thin wisp of smoke rose where the ball of yarn had been. Then the pillars moved apart again, and the prince slipped past them.

"Who are you looking for, my lad?" a voice asked.

"The Sun Princess."

"What is it you want of her?"

"I will tell her that when I see her."

"Are you here to woo the Princess?"

"What if I am!"

At this there came a tinkling laugh, but who it was that laughed the prince could not tell.

"Show the young man to the guest chamber," the voice said.

At once a whirlwind arose, and the prince was hurled on to the doorstep of a hut. The hut's thrice-nine doors of iron opened, and the prince found himself in a dungeon with a single tiny, heart-shaped window, close to the ceiling. There was no light other than came through this, and it was only when his eyes had got used to the darkness that the prince saw that he was not alone in the dungeon and that twenty-eight old men were there with him. Some of them were sitting on the floor, others were stretched out beside them with their heads resting on stones. Their long beards were matted, and their bodies frail and bent with age.

"Who are you and what are you doing here?" the prince asked.

"You can see for yourself what we look like now, but we used to be as young and as strong as you," one of them said. "We came here to woo the Sun Princess, and this is what has become of us. I have been here for a hundred and twenty-five years, and that man there, who is the oldest among us, for almost six hundred years. Our sufferings are without end, and there is nothing left us but to await death."

"Do not grieve," said the prince. "Surely we can free ourselves! There are twenty-nine of us, and we are brave men all."

But the old men only shook their heads and didn't utter a word.

All of a sudden there came a rap at the window, and someone threw some of oats into the dungeon. The old men jumped up and rushed to pick up the oats from the floor.

"Why don't you eat!" said they to the prince. "We won't get anything more."

"I am not a goose to peck at oats," said the prince.

"You won't say that when you go hungry long enough," the old men said, stuffing the oats into their mouths.

Someone now thrust a jug of water into the dungeon, but

the prince snatched up the jug and poured the water out of the window.

"What have you done!" the old men moaned. "Now we won't get any water to drink till tomorrow, and if the Sun Princess is angered, why, she'll not give us any, and we'll die of thirst."

"Don't be afraid! And throw the oats out too so that she stops treating you so."

And the prince snatched up a handful of oats and flung them out of the window.

The old men groaned, and falling to their knees, crawled about the floor and picked up the scattered oats grain by grain. Then the prince got out the silken kerchief Falcon had given him, and as if out of thin air, the most dainty dishes and the rarest of drinks appeared before him. The old men fell to and ate as if they could never have their fill. They drank the mead happily, thanked the prince again and again and called him their saviour.

Just then the Sun Princess's lady-in-waiting, Bright Dawn, peeked in at the window, and seeing Falcon's magic kerchief, went off in haste to tell the Sun Princess about it.

"I must have that kerchief! Tell him who brought it that he can have whatever he asks for it," said the Sun Princess.

Bright Dawn came back to the dungeon and asked the

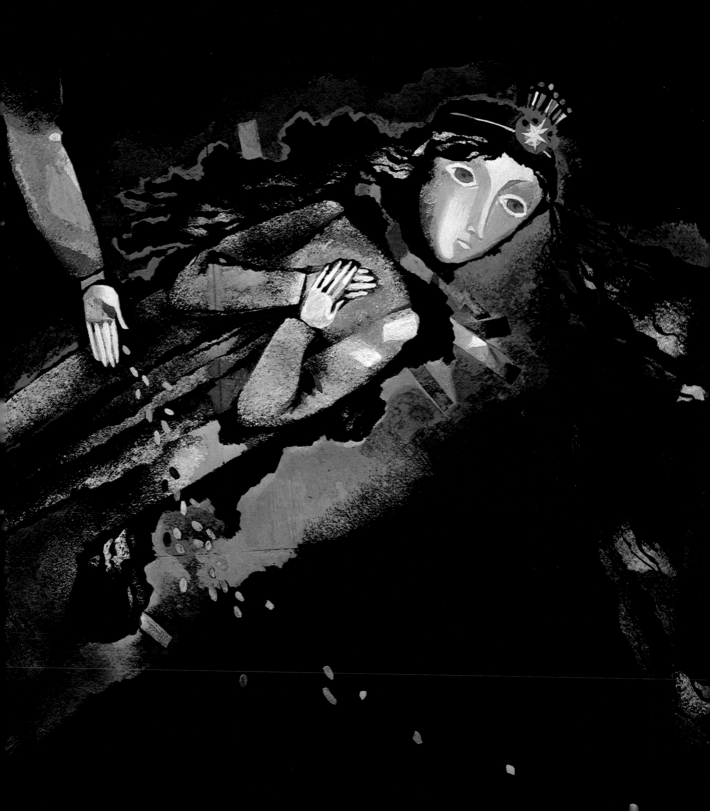

prince for the kerchief.

"Don't give it to her," the old men said. "If you do, it'll be the end of us, and of you, too, for you'll not have anything to eat but oats to your dying day."

But the prince would not listen to them.

"Come inside and take the kerchief," said he to Bright Dawn.

Bright Dawn did as the prince bade. She came into the dungeon, and so dazzling was her beauty that the old men were blinded by it and rushed to hide in dark corners.

Only the prince faced Bright Dawn unafraid.

"Tell the Sun Princess that the kerchief is hers and that I wish her health and happiness," said he.

Bright Dawn went back to the Sun Princess and gave her the kerchief, and the Sun Princess took it eagerly, but when she heard what the prince had said she only laughed. She spread out the kerchief, tried some of the dainty dishes, had a sip of the mead, and said:

"Now the man who gave me the kerchief will have nothing but oats to eat, like the rest."

But on the following day the prince again threw the oats that were brought to the dungeon out of the window, and the Sun Princess sent another of her ladies-in-waiting, Evening Star, to find out what this could mean. Evening Star peeked into the dungeon and saw that the old men were drinking wine and eating all kinds of dainty foods. Sounds of music came from the golden casket, and when the old men had eaten they began to dance.

Said Evening Star, and her voice came to them through the heart-shaped window in the wall:

"The Sun Princess commands you to sell her your casket, stranger!"

"Come in, and you shall have it," the prince said.

The thrice-nine doors opened, and Evening Star stepped inside. She was as lovely as her name betokened.

The old men fell at the prince's feet and implored him not to give up the magic casket, for, said they, they had tasted of wine again and of meat and could not bear the thought of going hungry.

But the prince would not listen to them. He asked Evening Star to sit down and he treated her to some mead and to the daintiest of the many dishes he set before her. Evening Star ate and drank, but when the time came for her to go back to the Sun Princess, she found that she could not get up! For the prince had smeared some of his magic porridge over the stone she was sitting on, and she was stuck fast to it! And though she threshed about wildly in an effort to get free, though she pleaded with the prince and wept bitter tears, he would not let her go. And as for the old men, they were as pleased as pleased

117

could be that she who had given them nothing but oats to eat for so many years was at last getting her due.

Now, the Sun Princess heard the singing and the music, but she could not understand why there was such merriment in the dungeon or why Evening Star had not returned. She decided to see for herself what had happened to her and came into the dungeon, and so dazzling was her beauty that the old men covered their eyes with their hands for fear of being blinded, and the Prince's heart missed a beat.

"Leave this place at once!" said the Sun Princess to Evening Star.

"Why should I, I'm happy where I am!" Evening Star returned. She had had more mead than was good for her.

"I'll not have such goings-on!" the Sun Princess cried and she turned to the prince. "Sell me your casket, stranger," said she.

"O loveliest of queens, you have stolen my heart from me!" the prince said. "Take whatever you wish—my casket, Evening Star here, or me, your obedient servant."

"I'll have all three," the Sun Princess said, and she held out her hand to the prince. She led him to her palace, seated him on the throne and said:

"I am the Sun Princess, and you shall be my husband. Here are the keys to all the forty rooms in my palace. You are free to go everywhere and to unlock thirty-nine of the doors, but if you want to have me always beside you, do not open the fortieth door."

The prince married the Sun Princess, made his home in her palace and was so happy that he forgot all about his brothers-in-law. But he freed the Sun Princess's twenty-eight captives, who crawled out of the dungeon and began kissing the ground under his feet. This the prince did not much like, he turned away and left them, and taking the keys his wife had given him, decided to see what there was to see in her palace.

He opened the first chamber and found the strangest of fishes there; he opened the second chamber, and there were birds there that sang in nine different voices; he opened the third chamber, and fearful beasts leapt out at him; he opened the fourth chamber and found winter there with her hoary breath and her fingers of ice; he opened the fifth chamber, and it was full of bright-winged butterflies and of grasshoppers dressed up in their green jackets. The palace sparkled and played, hummed and droned, for in it were all the colours, sounds and smells in which the earth abounds.

The prince marvelled at all this, but he could not make himself forget about the fortieth chamber. Surely the Sun Princess had been jesting when she forbade him to unlock it, he told himself, for nothing on earth could come between them and their love!

So one day the prince came up to the fortieth chamber and turned the key in the lock. The iron door opened with a creak.

The prince came inside and looked about him, but there was no one there and only a moss-grown pillar, with chains stretching from it to the room's four corners, rose in the centre of the floor. The prince touched the pillar and turned to go when he heard it sigh.

"Do take pity on me, my good youth!" it said in a human voice. "There is a tub of water in the corner. Scoop up some and let me have a drink, and I will reward you for your kindness."

The prince turned and saw a tub with a large ladle beside it. Picking up the ladle, he scooped up some water and gave it to the pillar. The pillar drank it and asked for more, and when the prince gave it more water, it swallowed it at a gulp. Then it shook itself, jangled its chains and asked for still more water. This it drank very, very quickly, and lo!—down fell the chains to the floor and off dropped the moss, the pillar straightened up, and the prince saw that it was not a pillar at all but a giant.

"Many thanks to you, my good youth!" he roared. "Now the Sun Princess will be mine!"

And soaring to the ceiling, as swiftly as a whirlwind, he rushed out of the chamber, caught up the Sun Princess and made off with her across the sky! For a moment or two the Sun Princess's fiery tresses flamed over the dark forest and then they, too, vanished and only a fading glow showed where the giant had gone.

The skies darkened, and it grew suddenly very cold. The crows hid under the burdocks, the flowers drooped and withered, and fear settled in the forests, in the seas and in people's homes.

But no one's heart was darker than the prince's, for had he not brought it all about himself! What was he to do? How was he to save the Sun Princess?

He thought and thought, and choosing the best horse in the royal stables, he rode off at a gallop after the giant who had stolen his wife and, with her, all his happiness.

On and on rode the prince for two whole days, and it was on the third day that he came to the giant's castle. He found the giant asleep and snoring loudly and three-eyed goat keeping watch over the Sun Princess.

The prince decided to try and put the goat to sleep, so down he sat and began singing a lullaby.

*Close your eye, goat,*
*Close your other eye!*

But he forgot all about the third eye. The goat closed two of his eyes, but he saw everything with the third one, and no sooner had the prince carried the Sun Princess over the wall and put her on his horse than he began bleating loudly.

"Wake up, giant, the prince has carried off the Sun Princess!" he cried.

And this he had to repeat three times before the giant opened his eyes.

"We've plenty of time," he said in his gruff voice. "We'll dig some potatoes first and then go after them."

The prince and the Sun Princess were far away when the giant, having dug a whole sackful of potatoes, got on the back of his three-eyed goat. Up to the clouds he soared and then dropped to the ground and seized the runaways.

"I will not kill you, for you gave me water to drink and brought me back to life," said he to the prince. "But never let me set eyes on you again or you'll fare badly."

And whistling loudly, he caught up the Sun Princess and rushed off with her on his goat before she had had time to do anything but throw a ball of yarn to the prince.

One disaster after another now descended upon the earth. A terrible rainstorm broke out and winds so fierce began to blow that they tore the roofs off houses, bent trees to the ground and swept baby birds out of their nests.

The prince again tried to carry off the Sun Princess, but this time, too, he forgot about the goat's third eye. He had put the Sun Princess on his horse and was riding away with her when

the goat began bleating loudly.

"The prince has carried off the Sun Princess again. Wake up, giant!" he cried.

The giant opened his eyes.

"Never you mind. We'll bake the potatoes we have dug and still have time to overtake them," he said.

The prince and his wife had just reached her palace when suddenly an icy wind began to blow, and their way was barred by the giant. The giant struck the prince on the head with his cudgel, and seizing the Sun Princess, who was more dead than alive, carried her off to his kingdom before she had had time to do anything but throw the prince her magic kerchief.

Once again evil times arrived, and confusion reigned throughout. Houses were buried in snow to the roofs, fires went out, and cold and hunger brought sickness in their wake.

The prince lay dead where the giant had left him, and the ravens dropped down from the sky and were about to peck out his eyes when lo!—there was Falcon flying up to him. He drove away the ravens, and bringing some living water from the Sun Princess's palace, sprinkled it over the prince.

The prince came back to life.

"I must free my wife!" he cried.

"You'll never free her, not while you ride an ordinary horse," Falcon said. "Go to Laume the Witch and get her to take you on as her herdsman. And do all her cat tells you to. The giant keeps his strength in the egg of a wild duck that lives by the side of the sea. You must ride the witch's horse there, catch the duck and take away the egg. And you have only to crack it for the giant to breathe his last. And now it is time for you to set out—the ball of yarn will guide you to Laume's land—and may good fortune attend you. Fear nothing. If ever you are in trouble, take out your kerchief, and I and your other brothers-in-law will come to your aid."

The prince threw down the ball of yarn and let it roll wherever it would. The ball of yarn rolled down the road, on and on it rolled for a day and another day, and on the third day it stopped by a hut. The hut was very old and covered with cobweb and only rats scuttled and dogs prowled about near it.

Laume the Witch met the prince at the door.

"Where are you going, my lad?" she asked.

"To seek someone who will give me some work to do."

"Stay with me and herd my twelve mares for three days. If you bring them safely home each evening you can have anything you ask for, but if even one is missing it'll be the end of you. And now come and have something to eat."

The prince sat down at the table and began to eat, and a cat jumped on his knee, and snuggling up against him, said:

"Give me a bit of the meat you are eating, prince, and I will help you."

The prince threw one of the choicest bits under the bench, and the cat ate it and said:

"The mares are all Laume's own daughters, prince. I'll go now and try to learn what trick they mean to play on you."

He went away but was soon back again, and he told the prince that the witch had ordered her daughters to turn into fishes and hide amid the weeds in the river.

Morning came, and Laume woke the prince, ordered him to drive the mares to pasture, and gave him a slice of cheese to take with him.

The prince pastured the mares in the forests, he pastured them in the meadows and on the banks of rivers, and they nibbled the grass and did not try to run away. But after a time the prince became very hungry, he ate the cheese Laume had given him and fell asleep. And the mares waded into the river and turned into fishes. The prince woke, he looked about him, but the mares were gone, and though he called to them not a sound did he hear in reply.

It was time to drive the mares home, and the prince began to fear that the witch would kill him for having lost them. Not knowing what to do, he took out his kerchief, and lo!—Pike appeared.

"What has Laume turned her daughters into, prince?" he asked.

"Fishes," said the prince.

Pike turned into a crayfish and went after the witch's daughters. He caught a fish, then another, and then a third, and he tore them to bits with his claws. After that what were the witch's daughters to do but turn back into mares again! The prince drove them home, and they stumbled wearily along, with hanging heads.

Laume met them at the gate and set to thrashing and beating them.

"Take that for not having listened to me!" she cried, seething with rage. "All you did was prance and run about!" And she added half under her breath:

"Never did any of my herdsmen get away from me alive, and this one won't, either!"

She scolded and beat her daughters all evening and then ordered them to turn into woodpeckers on the morrow and to hide in the hollows of trees. The cat heard her and told the prince about it, and the prince became sad and woebegone, for he did not know how he was to catch them.

On the following day he ate the cheese Laume had given him again and fell asleep, and the mares turned into woodpeckers and hid in tree hollows. He woke and began calling

132

them, but they did not show themselves, so he waved his kerchief, and lo!—Falcon came flying up to him. He turned into a hawk, and catching the woodpeckers, began tearing them to shreds. After that there was nothing the witch's daughters could do but turn back into mares, and the prince drove them home. Laume met them at the gate, she snatched the whip out of the prince's hands and set to beating the mares over their heads with it. And she shook with rage at their not having been able to hide themselves better.

"Who knows what the herdsman, rogue that he is, might ask me to give him!" she cried. "You worthless so-and-so's, you've disgraced our whole witches' family! Tomorrow you'll turn into grubs and hide under the bark of trees, and if you let him find you you'll pay with your lives for it!"

The cat heard her and passed it on to the prince, and the prince was so troubled that he could not sleep, for how was he to find the grubs.

But Falcon came to his aid again, he turned into a woodpecker, pecked at the bark and gouged out the grubs. For the third and last time the prince drove the mares, who kept whinnying piteously, home to their mother. Laume met them and she was in such a rage that she foamed at the mouth. She set to lashing and whipping her daughters and she called curses down upon their heads. Then she turned to the prince and said to him in a voice that dripped honey:

"Go and take a nap, and tomorrow you can choose whatever it is you set your heart on of all I have in my house."

"I want neither your rats nor your dogs," said the prince. "Give me the smallest of your fillies and I'll ask for nothing more."

"The smallest of my fillies? Why, she's on her last legs. Just look at her!"

The prince looked where she was pointing, and there, in a corner of the yard, he saw a filly no much bigger than a cat. She lay without stirring and seemed half-dead.

"What good is a jade like that to you!" Laume said. "She's sure to die before ever you get home, and all of your labours will have been wasted."

But the prince would not listen to her and lifted the filly in his arms. At this Laume began to shake as in a fever, for though the prince did not know it, the filly was her favourite grandchild and as strong as twelve mares.

The prince walked away with the filly in his arms, and she grew and became heavier at every step. After he had walked a mile the prince was able to get on her back, and when he had ridden her for eight miles, she spoke up in a human voice.

"Tell me where it is you want to go," she said.

"I must get to the seashore, catch a duck there and take her egg away from her," said the prince.

"So be it!" the filly cried, and soaring up to the sky so fast that her hoofs struck sparks from the clouds, away she flew!

Some time passed, and she dropped down, and now the sea lay at the prince's feet, and the waves flung pink shells and pieces of amber on to the beach.

Far out at sea, playing about in the water, was a speckled duck. The prince had neither bow nor crossbow with him, and he could not catch the duck with his bare hands, so down he sat on the white sand and burst into tears. But Pike thrust his head up out of the water and said:

"Do not weep, prince, I will catch the duck for you."

And though the duck screeched and threshed the water, it could not get away from Pike who dragged it to the prince. The prince tore it in two, took out the egg in which the giant's strength was kept, and thrusting the egg in his bosom, jumped on the filly's back. He rode to where he could see a fire burning and where he knew the giant's castle to be and was soon pounding away at the palace gate.

"I have come to free the Sun Princess!" he cried.

A cold wind began to blow, and the giant, his hair matted and uncombed, strode out of the gate, waving his cudgel.

"Out of my sight, worthless youth!" he roared. "If you don't go away at once I'll kill you, burn your body and cast the ashes into the wind!"

"That you will never do!" the prince said. "For I hold your strength and your very life in the palm of my hand."

He dashed the egg to the ground, the egg broke, and the giant dropped dead.

The Sun Princess came running out of the castle, she threw her arms round the prince, and lo!—the whole of the earth was flooded with light.

Then the Sun Princess flung her marriage belt, a rainbow, to the sky, and the prince held a feast in her honour. At this feast her laughter rang out and cheered all hearts as did the tales she recounted about true and faithful love. But the prince spoke of his parents, who, he said, were wasting away in their grief at there being no news of him for so long, and the Sun Princess felt sorry for them. She gave back their proper shape to Falcon, Bear and Pike, and telling her servants to have five chariots waiting at the gate, hurried out of the palace together with the prince and his sisters and brothers-in-law. They climbed into four of the chariots and rode off to pay the prince's mother and father a visit, and the fifth chariot rolled after them.

Now, if you are wondering who it was that rode in it, I'll tell you who. It was none other than New Moon, son of the Sun Princess and the prince, who was born soon after their happy reunion.

The book opens with the illustrations by the Latvian artist **Gunārs Krollis**. Krollis' unusual colour range is most attractive. His stylization does not obscure the national flavour of his drawing, but rather adds a special fairy-tale quality to it. Krollis has been showing his work at Republican, All-Union and international exhibitions since 1959. He has illustrated and designed more than eighty books, the best of which, in his opinion, are his illustrations for Charles Perrault's *Puss in Boots*.

In this book Krollis has done the drawings for two stories, *The White Deer* and *The Sea Bride*.

The young Estonian artist **Jaan Tammsaar** immediately attracted attention with his vivid and unusual style. He has frequently won awards at book design competitions, including three Best Baltic Book diplomas, a first class diploma at the All-Union Best Book of 1981 competition and the Jaan Jensen prize.

His illustrations for *The Forbidden Knot* and *The King of the Mushrooms* in this volume are both concrete and fantastic at the same time, as well as being extremely colourful.

The Lithuanian artist **Vange Gedmantaite-Galkuviene** works mainly with children's books. She has illustrated more than twenty books, including folk tales, songs and young children's stories by modern Lithuanian writers.

She first entered her work for the Republican book design exhibition at the age of twenty-five. Her drawings won an award, and since then her work has frequently won prizes not only in the Soviet Union, but also at major competitions abroad.

The artist's drawings for the Lithuanian folk tale *The Sun Princess and the Prince* are full of a mysterious charm which is achieved by her masterly colour combinations and unusual method of representation.

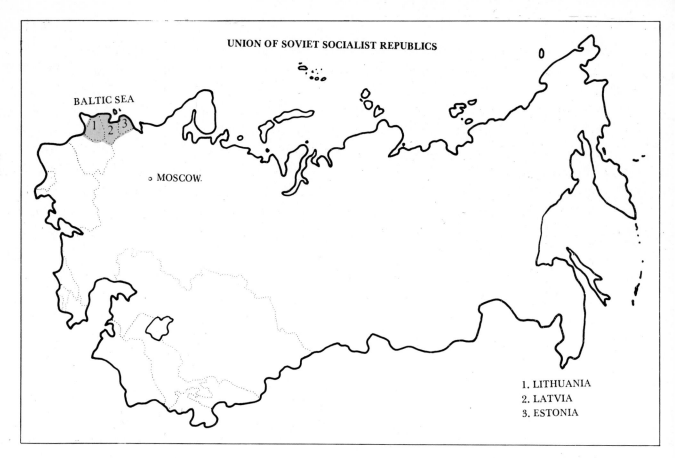

UNION OF SOVIET SOCIALIST REPUBLICS

BALTIC SEA

MOSCOW.

1. LITHUANIA
2. LATVIA
3. ESTONIA

The Soviet Baltic republics, Latvia, Lithuania and Estonia, are closely bound up with the sea. And the people who live there are what you would expect sea folk to be, tall, tough and strong. This is a land of fishermen, ship-builders and farmers. Each republic also has a highly developed industry. The radios, transmitters, etc. made in Latvia and Estonia are known throughout the world.

The proximity to the North Sea, the abundant forests and the austere beauty of the countryside have determined the main colours used in folk art. Unlike the southern republics of the Soviet Union where bright, vivid tones predominate, in the Baltic republics there is a preference for muted combinations, for colours that are in keeping with the surrounding countryside. The people here love wood and know how to use it. Even in the big towns many household articles are made of wood and it is often used for interior decoration.

Baltic amber is famous all over the world. The sea coast of Lithuania in particular abounds in it. This warm sun-like stone is used to create extraordinarily beautiful jewelry. Amber has also been used for centuries as a folk remedy that can cure various ailments and has health-giving properties. There is an Amber Museum in the town of Palanga, where you can admire the gleaming stones, some polished and carved by human hand, others given shape and colour by the hand of nature.

Baltic folk tales have absorbed much of the world around them, of course. They seem to smell of dry wood, resin, sea and forest. Many of the characters in the old songs and legends resemble the people of today who live in these parts: the wise fishermen, the skilled craftsmen, the sturdy, brave young men and the gentle, faithful women. The forces of evil in these stories take the form of terrible monsters, catastrophies and disasters which the heroes have to combat and overcome.

# REQUEST TO READERS

Raduga Publishers would be glad to have your opinion of this book, its translation and design and any suggestions you may have for future publications.

Please send all your comments to 17, Zubovsky Boulevard, Moscow, USSR.

Сказки народов Прибалтики

СКАЗКИ НАРОДОВ СССР

*На английском языке*

© Состав, справки о художниках, текст о республиках. Издательство "Радуга", 1986 г.

*Printed in the Union of Soviet Socialist Republics*

$$C \frac{4803000000-143}{031(01)-87} \text{ без объявл.}$$